GIBBONS
A Strange
Land

With illustrations by
Alan Brown

To Malala Yousafzai, an inspirational woman

First published in 2015 in Great Britain by
Barrington Stoke Ltd
18 Walker Street, Edinburgh, EH3 7LP

www.barringtonstoke.co.uk

This story was first published in a different
form in *Skin Deep* (Penguin, 2004)

Text © 2004 Alan Gibbons
Illustrations © 2015 Alan Brown

The moral right of Alan Gibbons and Alan Brown to be
identified as the author and illustrator of this work has been
asserted in accordance with the Copyright, Designs and
Patents Act, 1988

A CIP catalogue record for this book is available
from the British Library upon request

ISBN: 978-1-78112-432-1

Printed in China by Leo

Contents

Chapter 1
Ropes

There are these people. They've got something on me.

I'm Jack Keenan. In turn, I've got something on one of the refugee boys.

He's called Hassan. Hassan is new, so he doesn't have anything on anybody. He's just trying to learn the ropes. He wants to fit in, but it isn't that easy. Not at my school. That's the way it is with new kids. They're outside the loop. Unprotected.

That's what makes Hassan the weakest link. He's the one that can be broken. He's the one they've ordered me to break.

Chapter 2
Inner Circle

I seem to have started in the middle of my story so maybe it's best to jump back to the start.

I guess I better explain about the people who have got something on me. The people who are blackmailing me. They're called the Blokes. The Blokes are maybe half a dozen kids, ten at most, who pull the strings at my school. You wouldn't think so few kids could be so powerful, but the Blokes are.

The Blokes say what's OK and what's not. Who gets dragged into the inner circles, who is kept out, who is to be broken. And they've decided that Hassan has to be broken.

So be it.

The main thing about the Blokes is that they are English. Add that to the fact that they are white and, well, blokes, and you pretty much have it. Girls are for show only. Totty. As for the black kids and the refugees, they'll never be part of the inner circle. The inner circle is for whites only.

For the Blokes, English equals white.

'There ain't no black in the Union Jack. Or brown.'

That's what the Blokes think. The bottom line is, the Blokes like to think they are as English as fish and chips, St George T-shirts and a thump in the kidneys.

Chapter 3
Pride

I only became aware of the Blokes at the start of the autumn term this year, but it seems they got set up when the first refugees arrived – when they entered our school. That's when the graffiti started, little St George flags with their name written over the top – The Blokes.

Most people thought it was some sort of pop group at first, then we started to hear about the penalties.

There's this kid in Year 7, Calvin Chong. As far as I can make out, he was the first victim. He's brainy, quiet and good at music, which is three strikes against him as far as the Blokes go. Plus, his mum and dad come from China.

At the end of November, Calvin won the Head Teacher's Award for Music and his whole family came to a special Assembly to watch him get given it. Everyone could see how proud they were of Calvin – the pride was just pouring out of them.

I bet that's what did it – that show of pride. At the start of December, Calvin got an early Christmas present. The Blokes scared one of Calvin's friends into handing over his clarinet.

That's how they work – they play kids off against each other. Divide and rule. When the Blokes got their hands on that clarinet they chucked it on the floor and stamped on it. By the time it got back to Calvin, it was in bits.

The Chongs came in to complain, but all that happened as a result of that was that the Blokes worked Calvin over a couple of times. When they flushed his head down the boys' toilet, that put a stop to the complaints.

That pride of theirs, it didn't do the family any good. Calvin was victim number one, but I know he won't be the last.

Chapter 4
Targets

Since they carried out that first strike against Calvin, the Blokes have been more and more active. It got so bad that one Sikh family even took their kids out of here and moved them to a school that treats stuff like this seriously. That was two weeks ago. We all watched them go on their last day.

We felt sorry for them and bad about what had happened, but we couldn't help feeling glad we weren't in their shoes.

I know what you're thinking – what do I need to worry about? I'm white, English, so why would the Blokes pick on me? But that's the whole point. The way it works is like this. There are three camps in school –

There are the Blokes.

There are the Blokes' targets – the black kids, the Asian kids and the refugees.

Then there's the rest – the white kids that just want to keep their heads down and survive.

And that's why the Blokes have got me in their sights. I'm one of the quiet kids who try to go with the flow. I don't have anything against anybody. The trouble is, in the Blokes' eyes, no one can sit on the fence. Andy Lyons is the Blokes' big cheese, and one time he said to me, "You're either with us or you're against us." And I dared to make friends with Hassan, so I was against them until I proved I wasn't.

So, I reckon you're wondering, 'What's the big deal? Hassan's your friend. Tell the Blokes to take a running jump. OK, so they might give you a bit of hassle. Big deal. It's not the end of the world.'

But it isn't that easy. Life never is. It's like I tried to explain before. The Blokes have got something on me. Something big.

Chapter 5
Kid

The something big that the Blokes have got on me is my dad.

My dad killed a kid.

He didn't mean to. He was doing 30 in a 30 miles-per-hour zone near our old house. He wasn't speeding. The kid just stepped out. Nothing Dad could do.

But it doesn't matter if Dad's innocent,
does it? The kid's family couldn't accept that
it wasn't his fault. They started following him,
making threats. I can understand it, I suppose.
They'd lost their little boy. They needed
someone to blame. But it made life hard for
us. Mum wanted to stay and stick it out. But
Dad wouldn't listen to her. He'd had enough.

He wanted to get away. That's why we moved house and I ended up at my new school.

So there you go. That's what the Blokes have got on me. My mate Josh spilled his guts to them.

Here's what Andy Lyons said to me the day after.

"A little birdy tells me your dad's a murderer."

Yes, just like that. I looked round at the other kids in the corridor, but they didn't hear. They were keeping well clear. Well, you would if you saw Andy Lyons and two of his heavies corner somebody. I checked again to make sure nobody was listening, then I stared at Andy. I was willing him to keep his voice down.

"What?" I said.

"You heard me," Andy said. "A kid-killer. How low can you get?"

"He didn't do anything wrong," I said. "It was an accident."

My skin was burning all the way down my spine. My heart flipped over in my chest. I knew that the Blokes had their claws in me. I belonged to them now. Can you imagine what that's like? I seemed to have toppled right off the edge of the world.

Andy smirked. "Sure." He chuckled. "An accident. That's what they all say."

Now his acid words were burning me down to the bone. I was dying of shame. Dad's shame.

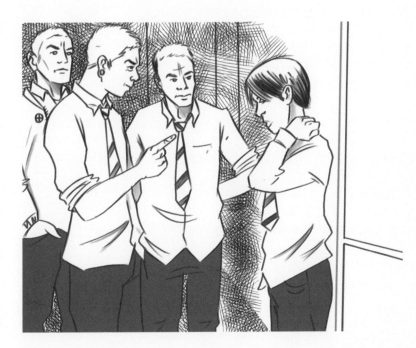

"It's true," I told him. "It was an accident."

"True or false," Andy said. "You don't want it to get round. A kid-killer for a dad. Can't be good for the image, can it? But we can keep quiet about it, of course. It can be our little secret, can't it?"

"What do you want?" I asked.

"Nothing just now," Andy said. "But don't worry. I'll call in the favour." He took a few steps away, then looked back at me.

"Soon," he said.

Chapter 6
Gold

So that's how things stood. Until two weeks ago. That's when Mrs Fleming came up with her big idea to make the new kids welcome, the refugees from Syria.

Mrs Fleming's big idea was a competition called "Where I'm From". The plan is you make something – a poster, a map, a model, a sculpture – that shows off your roots. Jenny Bruce was born in Glasgow and she decided to make the St Andrew's flag out of a mosaic

of bits of coloured paper. Josh Lenahan is a
Scouser so he's making a Liver Bird out of
papier-mâché. I won't bore you with the rest.
You've got the picture by now. The point is,
everybody knows who is going to win.

Hassan.

He's brilliant with his hands. You've never seen anything like it. He's like that famous King Midas guy – everything he touches turns to gold.

Most of the kids think Mrs Fleming made up the competition just for Hassan. Like she thinks it might be a good way to make him feel more at home here.

She's got a point. The Syrians have a hard time. The council stuck them in a run-down tower block over on the north side of town and they've had nothing but aggro. Mrs Fleming wants to make amends, but I'm not sure she's done Hassan any favours. The Blokes have got wind of the whole thing and they plan to come down hard on him.

Which is where I come in.

Hassan trusts me, you see. We play football together and we've become big mates. Hassan

even asked if he could keep the model he's
building for the competition at my house. I live
closer to the school so there's less chance it'll
get damaged on the way. Of course he really
means there's less chance it'll get damaged
by some of the characters on his estate. Plus,
his flat is so poky you can't swing a cat, never
mind build a village.

That's what he's doing, by the way. He's
building a scale model of his village, the one
he left back in Syria. Soldiers came in trucks
and opened fire on the villagers and then they
looted and torched the 1,000-year-old mosque.
That's all Hassan will say, but I know he saw
stuff, bad stuff. The kind of stuff the Blokes
probably dream of doing one day.

I'm really scared that the Blokes will find out where Hassan keeps his village because I know what they'll do to it. And when they do, they'll remind me that whoever isn't with them is against them.

Then they'll make me betray my friend.

Chapter 7
Model

I'm in the playground at home time, waiting for

Hassan, when I hear Andy Lyons's voice.

"Hey Piggy," he says. "How's the model

coming on?"

The Blokes call Hassan "Piggy", you see, as

in "The Three Little Pigs". Because the pigs had

houses made of sticks and straw and all that.

It's a rubbish joke, but they think they're really

witty. Plus it is even more of an insult because Hassan is Muslim.

'Ignore them, Hassan,' I think. 'Don't talk to them. Just keep walking.'

"The model is good," Hassan says, with a shy smile. He knows not to trust Andy Lyons, but maybe he thinks Andy's turned over a new leaf. Fat chance. He's a Bloke.

"Yes?" Andy says, and he looks over at me. "Tell me about it."

"I used modelling clay," Hassan explains. "From the modelling clay I made mountains."

"Mountains, eh?" Andy says, with a nasty

glint in his eyes.

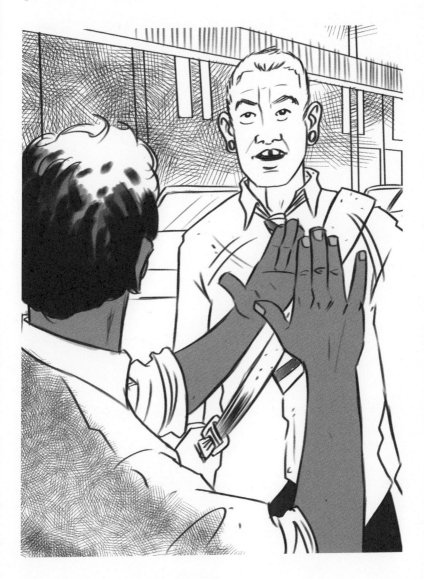

"Yes, I cover them with a brown fabric so that they look real. And on the mountains I have built tiny houses. They look like ..."

Hassan looks at me for the word.

"Boxes," I say. "Little boxes."

"Yes," Hassan says, and I see he likes the sound of the word. "Boxes."

"So you're going to paint them?" Andy asks.

"Yes," Hassan says. "The houses will be white. They will stand out against the brown of the mountains. And I will have a mosque at the end of the main street."

"Right," Andy says, and he nudges one of his mates in the ribs. "A mosque."

Hassan frowns. His smile has gone.

"I'm going now," he says. "With Jack."

"Yes, that's right," Andy says. "You run along with your good friend Jack."

Hassan frowns again. And I do too.

Chapter 8
Heart

An hour later I'm helping Hassan paint the houses. He has brought these really fine brushes from home. My hand won't keep still and I almost mess it up.

"No," says Hassan, kind but firm. "You must go slow, like this."

Hassan smiles. He has made some good stuff before, but this is his masterpiece. He made the other models with his hands and his brain. I think this village comes straight from his heart.

*

"I hear you're helping Piggy with his model," Andy says the next day.

"His name is Hassan," I say.

"I know what he's called," Andy says. "And you know what you're going to do."

"Do I?"

Andy brings his face close to mine. "You really want me to spell it out?" he asks.

No, I don't want him to spell it out. I know the Blokes want me to destroy Hassan's model.

When I don't answer, Andy pulls out a box of matches from his pocket.

"Let's say this is one of Hassan's little houses," he says. "Well. We were wondering what was wrong with English houses."

"Hassan doesn't come from England," I say, as if things are that simple.

"So, this is what you're going to do for us," Andy says, and he rests the little box on his palm. "You're going to take every one of

Piggy's cute little houses ... and you're going to squash them flat."

Andy puts the box down on the table and crushes it with his fist. He grins.

"After all," he says, "we don't want your daddy to get a bad name, do we?"

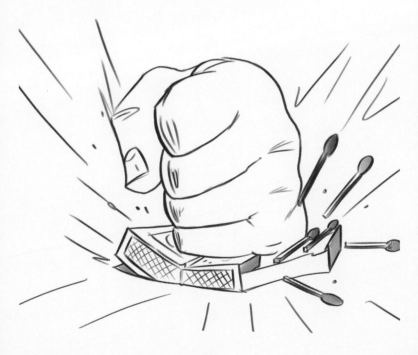

Chapter 9
Moonlight

I don't sleep too well that night.

After an hour of tossing and turning I get up and go downstairs. I go in the back room and look at Hassan's village. We finished the houses this evening. We just have the mosque to go.

The eerie light of a full moon falls on the white walls of the houses and they glow against the dark mountains. I try to imagine what it was like when the soldiers came. Hassan told me that they came after dark, on a moonlit night, a night just like this one. I look at the village and imagine the running feet, the bursts of gunfire, the fires and blasts from the grenades. I imagine the soldiers blowing the houses down, flattening them just like the Big Bad Wolf.

I'm still thinking these thoughts when Dad appears.

"What's up, son?" he says. "Can't sleep?"

I shake my head.

"Anything on your mind?" he asks. "I
know what it's like. I've had my fair share of
sleepless nights." He means the accident of
course.

"No," I say. "Nothing wrong."

I could get good at lying.

*

The next day Andy is waiting at the school gates. When he finds out that I haven't done it yet, that Hassan's model is still in one piece, he reminds me what the Blokes want.

"Competition day tomorrow," he says. "Tonight's the night."

"I know," I say.

"Just checking," says Andy.

He gives me a long, hard look, as if he's mulling something over, then he walks off with his mates.

Next thing, Hassan joins me.

"Can I come round to finish the mosque?" he asks. "It's my last chance to get it right. Competition day tomorrow."

"Yes," I say. "I know."

Chapter 10
Crushed

Hassan and I are putting the finishing touches to the mosque at about 7.30 p.m.

"Was the roof really gold?" I ask. I'm watching Hassan as he applies the second coat of gold paint with great care.

"No," Hassan says. "But it should have been."

I can't think of anything to say, so I
change the subject. "We'll be finished in a few
minutes," I say.

The evening light is falling on the village,
just like the moonlight did last night. It was
the soldiers I could see in the dark then.
Now, by the light of the setting sun, I can see

mothers putting their kids to bed, farmers on their way home from the fields.

'I'm sorry, Hassan,' I think. 'So sorry.'

Hassan looks at me and I wonder if I've spoken out loud.

"You're quiet," he says.

"Yes," I say.

My throat is so tight it's hard to speak. Just then Dad pops his head round the door and offers Hassan a lift home.

*

Ten minutes later I've got tears in my eyes and a big, black hole inside me. The houses are crushed, the shell of the mosque split in two. I've done it. I've done the Blokes' dirty work. I stand there staring at the ruins of the model until Dad comes in to see if I want some supper.

"Jack!" he cries. "What have you done?"

I start making excuses, but there's no point trying to pretend to him – so I explain and every bit of shame and horror comes tumbling out.

"Oh, Jack," Dad says. He shakes his head.

"You mean, you think I did the wrong

thing?" I say.

He nods. "I know you did."

"But they would have told," I say. "Everybody at school would know what you did."

"So what?" Dad says.

I can't believe what I'm hearing.

"Look, son," Dad says. "I was wrong. I should have stayed and stood up for myself, the way your mum wanted me to. And that's what you need to do now. You've got to phone Hassan and tell him what you've done."

Chapter 11
Broken

I try to argue with Dad, but he's having none of it. When at last I phone Hassan and tell him, his voice dies at the end of the line. He hangs up without a word. Then, ten minutes later, he's back on the phone.

"I will come round at 7.30 in the morning," he says. "I have things to do."

"But it's ruined," I say. "Broken to bits. I'm so sorry ..."

"Do the mountains still stand?" Hassan asks.

"Yes, but ..."

"Then I will be round early."

*

The next morning, Hassan doesn't want me in the room. I don't blame him.

"What's he doing?" Mum asks.

I shrug.

Hassan's face is like a mask. His eyes are like black stones. But he isn't beaten. That's what I don't understand. I can't get my head round it. The Blokes haven't broken him the way they broke me.

"Hassan," I say, and I knock on the door. "Can I help?"

"No," he says. "Just give me some more time."

It is 8.45 when at last Hassan opens the door. I can't see what he's done. The model is inside two black bin bags held together with sticky tape.

"Are we late?" he asks.

"Don't worry about that," Mum says. "I'll give you a lift in."

I can tell that she's impressed by Hassan and disappointed in me. Which makes the weight of shame inside of me even heavier.

Whatever Hassan has done, he's chosen to face up to the Blokes.

*

It is 11.30 and people are setting up their models in the school hall. The Blokes are watching. Andy tries to catch my eye, but I stare straight through him.

I go over to Hassan, hoping he doesn't tell me to leave him alone.

"But what have you done?" I ask. "There wasn't time to rebuild it."

"No," says Hassan, his voice cold and distant. "I didn't try."

Then, without another word, he removes the bin bags from around his model.

Mrs Fleming hesitates for a moment then says, "Oh, Hassan."

The shell of the mosque is still broken. The houses are still crushed. But Hassan has

rubbed charcoal into the white walls so that they look charred, as if by fire. He has removed what was left of the roofs and left the concrete homes open to the sky. Finally, here and there, he has pasted on red and orange tissue paper so that it looks like flames are licking the shattered buildings. Little donkeys, that I watched him carve leg by tiny leg from wood, lie dead on the road.

"This is my village," Hassan says. He meets the eyes first of Mrs Fleming then of Andy. "This is the truth."

Chapter 12
Truth

Five days later, the Blokes haven't said a word about Dad. Maybe they will and maybe they won't. I'm not sure it matters. They know I'm ready to tough it out. So is Dad. You can only scare someone who is ready to be scared. As for Hassan, I'm going bowling with him tonight. That was his prize for winning the competition with his village.

When he asked me to go with him, I couldn't believe it.

"You mean we're still friends?" I said. "After what I did?"

You know what Hassan said then?

"It was your hands that broke the village," he told me. "But they were moved by the badness in the hearts of others."

It seems the Blokes got Hassan wrong.

He isn't the weakest link.

He's the strongest.

I might not be the strongest, not by a long shot, but I'm going to learn from this, from

Hassan. I won't do the easy thing. I'll do the right thing. I'm hoping the Blokes got me wrong too – me and my dad. At least, I'll try to show them that they did. And maybe my prize will be staying friends with Hassan.